MacKenzie Smiles, LLC, San Francisco, CA

www.mackenziesmiles.com

Originally published as *Prinses Arabella is Jarig*
Copyright © 2006 Uitgeverij De Eenhoorn bvba,
Vlasstraat 17, B-8710 Wielsbeke
www.eenhoorn.be

Original text & artwork by Mylo Freeman

Art production by Ana Cachão

ISBN 978-0-9815761-7-6

Printed in China

10 9 8 7 6 5 4 3 2 1

Distributed in the US and Canada by:
Ingram Publisher Services
One Ingram Blvd.
P.O. Box 3006
LaVergne, TN 37086
(866) 400-5351

Mylo Freeman

Princess Arabella's
Birthday

Once upon a time, there was a little princess named Arabella. She lived in a big palace with her father and mother, the king and queen. Her birthday was nearly here. But what do you give a princess who already has everything?

"My dearest Arabella," the king said,
"what would you like for your birthday?"

Princess Arabella thought and thought.

"What about a pair of ruby roller skates?"
the queen asked.

"No," Arabella answered. "I already have those."

"A gold bicycle?"

"No," the princess answered.

"A cuddly mouse?"

"No," the princess answered.

"A tea set?"
"No."

"A rocking zebra?"
"No!"

"A stroller for your doll?"
"No!"

"I already have all of those things!" Princess Arabella screamed. "I want something different this year!"

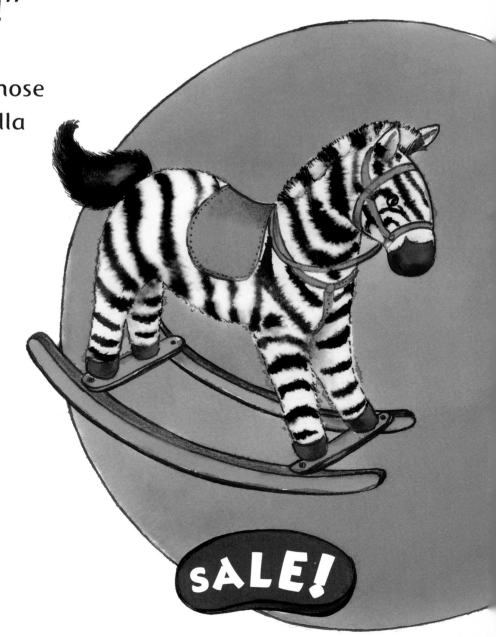

SALE!

"I want. . . an elephant!" the princess demanded.

"An ele. . . what?" the queen asked.

"But Arabella," said the king as he caught the fainting queen, "where would we keep such a large animal? And who would clean up after it and take it for walks?"

Princess Arabella waved away any objections. She wanted an elephant.

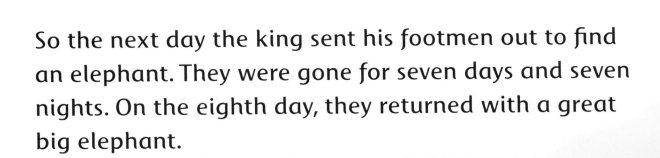

So the next day the king sent his footmen out to find an elephant. They were gone for seven days and seven nights. On the eighth day, they returned with a great big elephant.

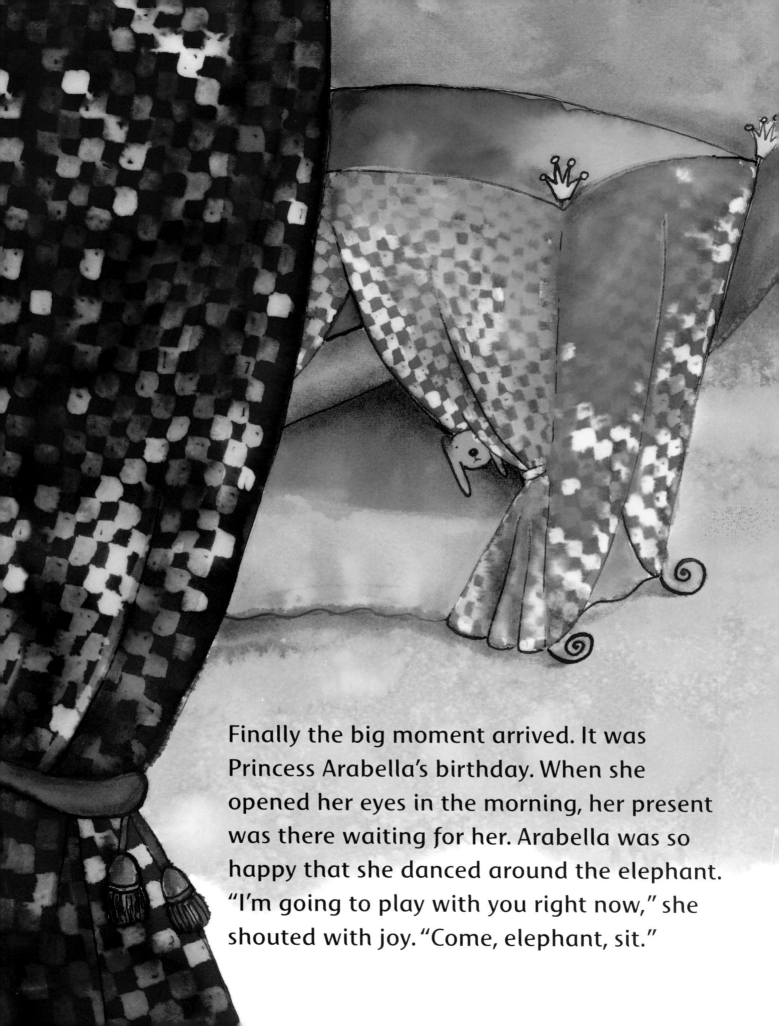

Finally the big moment arrived. It was Princess Arabella's birthday. When she opened her eyes in the morning, her present was there waiting for her. Arabella was so happy that she danced around the elephant. "I'm going to play with you right now," she shouted with joy. "Come, elephant, sit."

The elephant just stood there looking sad.

"Hey, you are my present! You have to play with me!" Arabella said impatiently.

But the elephant didn't move. A huge tear slowly ran down her trunk, and then another one and another one. It didn't take long before Princess Arabella was up to her ankles in tears. "Stop it," she said, "or soon I will drown!"

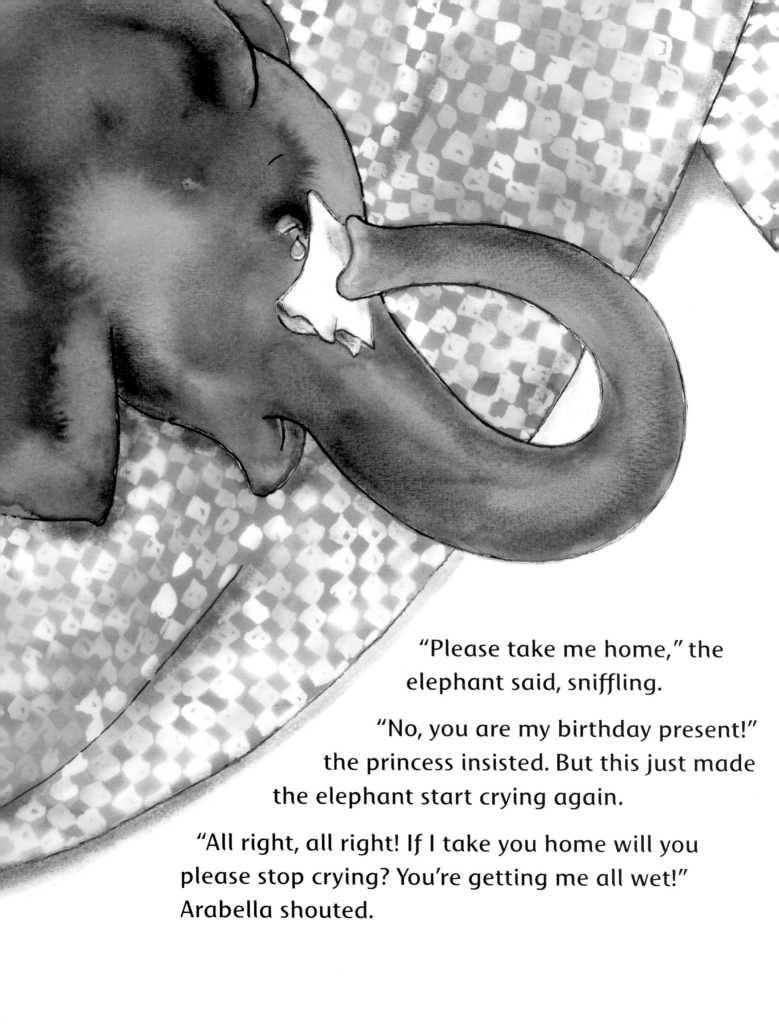

"Please take me home," the elephant said, sniffling.

"No, you are my birthday present!" the princess insisted. But this just made the elephant start crying again.

"All right, all right! If I take you home will you please stop crying? You're getting me all wet!" Arabella shouted.

And so they set out together. Along the way, Princess Arabella saw many amazing animals.

"Stop! I want that, and that, and that one, too!" she called to the elephant. But the elephant just kept going.

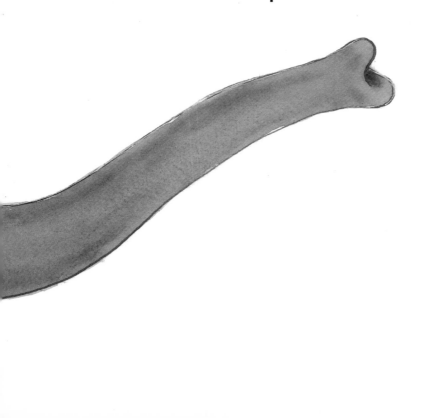

When they finally arrived at the place where the elephant lived, a tiny elephant came running toward them. "Mommy!" she said. "You are back just in time and you have my birthday present with you!"

"Yes, sweetheart," the elephant answered,
"and it is exactly what you wanted:
a real, little princess!"